Simon

Words: Jesse S. Mitchell

Illustrations: Håkan Eklund

Chapter One:
The Sunflower Story

Nothing really quite captures the quiet of life, the soundless expanse of undisturbed air that surrounds, the brief breezy notes that flutter nearly unnoticed past unappreciative ears. There are not proper words to describe it and there are not proper shapes or images to illustrate it. No songs or stories or murals, novels or films that bring it close. The truth is, everywhere is exceedingly quiet and beneath the quiet, carefully concealed, is everything…all the noises and colors and living creatures. A super still surface of sound, a glassy still surface like water. Touch it and it makes ripples, hit it and it makes splashes, jump in and it makes a reverberation, a crash, a hum…echoes riding outward toward the ends of the Earth, past the limits of sight, round Planets, cosmos, cold dying stars and bending, blending refracted light, and comes back and thuds hard against the side of your head with a distinct ring.

Simon is about to make a ripple. Sitting on his crisscrossed legs and barefoot in the dry, brown, cracked, over-tall grass, he looks to his left and counts the copper pipes stacked up in a haphazard pyramid. They are collecting heat and reflecting light. He has just finished digging deep into the awful, dusty, hard ground. A perfectly round hole, sides steep. Inside the hole he piled little rocks and gravel. He mixed up rock powder, dirt and water. He made a deep red paste and filled the hole flush and let it dry…mostly. Before it could set forever he grabbed the longest copper pipe and jabbed it hard into the mixture. He twisted it and put direct pressure on the top, driving it in deeper. He wiped off his hands and stood up, admired the dark green-red patina on the surface of all the different lengths of pipe…every one a slightly different color, a slightly different size, but he would make them fit together.

Behind him he could hear noises, animal sounds coming from far down the tree, vine and moss covered/infested old abandoned lane. There once were houses down that way, stores, buildings…nothing now but green overgrown nature and a sprinkling of yellow reflective eyes and feral sounds…enough to drive a young boy's imagination crazy. He never went down that way. He wasn't allowed and he had no desire anyway. Life had taken over. It was frightening, especially when you remember just what life can do.

He screwed a long thin pipe onto the one he had planted in the ground, and then another and another, using the longest and thinnest at first. The fine yellow dust of the lower Midwest/upper South flooded into his mouth and choked him. It collected in the corners of his eyes and under his ragged fingernails. He pinched himself screwing and screwing and banging pipes together and instinctively put the offended digit in his mouth. The grit felt like sandpaper and tasted like sawdust and alluvium. He swatted at time-traveling insects that could pop in and out of existence with every swipe of his exasperated hands. He had bites up and down his back, patches of sweat and purple-brown leg bruises.

It wasn't long before the pipes reached high into the sky and Simon had to retreat to a little goat shed to retrieve a rickety ladder. The ladder was missing most of the upper rungs. Simon broke off pieces of dead and dying tree branches that littered the sides of the tan-brown field and carefully jammed them into the slots that once held the perfectly manufactured ladder rungs. He tested them with his hands, putting pressure on each one until he felt safe. He climbed the ladder, a bundle of extremely hot and bulky pipes under his right arm, reached the top and laid the pile gingerly at the top of the ladder. He vigilantly and artfully began making two divergent lines of tubes, one going right and one going left. He climbed up another step and then another and finally he stood teetering at the very top. He wavered in the air, waiting to regain complete balance. He looked around and watched clouds go slowly by, listened to birds, some singing, some screeching. Looking down he thought he saw a snake. Nervously he waited…just a stick. He connected the two sets of pipes at the top, bent and shaped the whole construction and fashioned it into a circle, then climbed down again.

Walking slowly beneath the trees, he collected leaves, only the biggest and best and only the triangle shaped ones and only if they had a long stem still attached. He filled his turned up shirt with them and climbed back up the ladder. He pulled out a leaf at a time and weaved it delicately around the joints of the pipes. Only around the joints at first but then everywhere, he weaved the leaves together and to the whole circular structure.

Finally he was out of leaves and he was out of pipes and the whole thing was done and he climbed down. He stood in front of the figure and watched. He waited. He stood there for barely a fraction of a second (but it felt like a lifetime) when at last a tiny glow began to emanate out of the very center of the circle, slowly at first, but soon it grew and everywhere was bathed in bright yellow golden light. The circle blazed like a star. Simon stood in the light and cast no shadow. Everywhere was brilliant again. Everywhere was ignited again. Simon picked up a handful of the dust.

And this is how Simon restarted the sun.

And this is how Simon made his splash.

Chapter Two:
Demeler la Lune

Walking down the hillside from his home was always difficult, especially when it was shady and it was hard to see. You had to watch every step for thorns and vines. And then came the big trees, six or eight giant ancient trees that covered the whole lower side of the hill. All of this coming to an almost abrupt end at the silvery little strand of water, too big to be a stream because you couldn't cross it on your own.

Tonight was the same, difficult, maybe even a bit more awkward. Simon had already cut up his toes in places, little streaks of blood along the sides of his feet. So many birds out, tonight. A lot of noise.

In the low moss green grass, sticking out of the ground, was half a book. The cover gone and most of the pages. Peeking out was a light blue page, an architectural drawing. He passed for a few seconds and looked at it. It fluttered as he moved the air. It was big. It was a cathedral or a castle or a skyscraper. It didn't matter, it was beautiful. So precise. So clean. All the symbols and numbers and perfect straight lines danced together and curved around and billowed like smoke and filled the whole margins up.

He stumbled down to the muddy edges of the river, big dark green leaves above his head. The mud between his toes an ugly yellow tan, all clay and crushed up rocks. The canopy above him, dark green waxy leaves on one side, veinless plush silver petals on the other, vines and tall bushes scattered everywhere.

He stands for a while, his feet up to his ankles in the rippling water, squinting up through the trees at the little spots of light breaking through. It makes the surface of the water flash and it casts a checkerboard pattern of shade and color on all the vegetation. He thinks for a minute and rolls one of the errant fallen logs under his foot. He climbs up the bank a bit. A slick, bright green frog stops him. He gets eye level with the amphibian and closely examines the golden rings around its big bulging eyes. The strangest shade of color he had ever seen, a variation. Simon paused to consider nuance for a moment and then began yanking wildly but purposefully at some of the bigger, stronger vines. He piled them up and collected a few of the less waterlogged bits of braches and thicker pieces of wood. And after many tries, a few minor injuries and a couple of scares, he successfully lashes the whole thing together into a workable raft. He flops it down in the water and watches. The water splashes up in a cascade of tiny, foamy drops and…the raft floats. Simon sets both feet on board at once, brassily grabs a long floating stick off the surface of the water and propels himself to the other side of the creek. Into the forest.

The forest was another matter entirely. It was always dark and shady in the woods. It was obviously filled with wild animals. The signs of them were everywhere: a feather, a clump of hair, droppings, shed skins and shed antlers…but you never saw anything and there was never a sound. Complete silence. When Simon inched off the raft and scampered up the opposite bank, he did so warily. Simon had been in these woods before many times, but never for amusement and never with a hope of ever returning.

He walked anxiously between the trees, the dark grey trunks of trees. They looked like the pillars and columns in old-fashioned temples, Egyptian and Greek. He deliberately stepped and chose every move carefully, his feet crunching year-old, dried out, nearly petrified leaves. Snapping twigs and rolling mossy rocks.

He finally made it to the tree in the middle. A great big giant tree, trunk massive, canopy astounding. Leaves everywhere, dripping down right above Simon's head. Every time he breathed the most incredible thing happened. Each breath he took, in or out, caused a tiny breeze to blow across the leaves and make a hypnotic swooshing sound. He walked up to the trunk of the tree. It had rough, dry bark that would come off in big strips if you pulled on it. Simon sometimes pulled on it, but not often and not in quite awhile. He didn't think it was right that he should. The ground was warm here and the tree's big roots jutted out from under the ground in places and big patches of moss grew on them, hanging upside down off the odd curves and arches. Simon noticed there was a faint kind of light coming from behind the tree, an outline but without lines…a glow but without dissipation.

He walked around the tree. He circled around and stood in front of a knot of skinny grey branches going every direction. They looked like arms and legs, bent in rough patches like knuckles and knees. Deep inside the twist and snarl of wood, a deep but pale phosphorescent white light glimmered. Simon could see it in places and if he moved this way or that, he could see more of it. He stared at it, deeply into, became transfixed by it. He walked up closer, practically climbed up the side of the great tree, tried to see the thing from all angles. He walked back and considered for a minute the problem. Rubbed his chin. Paced. Lastly, he ran violently upon it and grabbed chaotically at a few of the bottom limbs and began yanking, pulling with all his might, replacing his grip occasionally and reaching for higher branches and ones on further back or deeper inside. And after a few minutes of madly assaulting the seemingly immovable branches of steel, they began to shift…and groan. And slowly but surely, like a flower bud expanding into bloom, the branches fanned out and released.

There it is was, a perfect spherical luminance, burning like strange fire.

Simon stared at it, mouth agape. The ball rose into the air and grew bigger and bigger as it further elevated itself. Cold white moonlight flooded everything. And the tree leaves fluttered relief. And the breeze swooshed the grass and the forest canopy. Simon reached down and picked up a handful of the moist dark earth.

And this is how Simon untangled the moon.

It was easier to see going back up the hillside near his house now, not just this night but all nights from then on, and he hardly ever cut up his feet anymore.

Chapter Three:
Simon the Wind God

Simon walked out his front door early in the morning. Little strips of peeled white paint from the disintegrating screen door still clinging to his palms. Tranquil but not serene. The sky was so low and overcast that the trees reached up and clawed at the belly of the thing. When his bare feet stepped down on the bright green yard, he thought he could hear it squeak. It felt like there were little drops of something wet crowding him but not touching him. It made him uncomfortable. And it made him squint. The sun looked funny today, diffused and scattered. His eyes didn't like this. This caused him to stop for awhile and ponder on why that was…never landing on an acceptable explanation, Simon set out walking. He went past the tall hedges with the stiff leaves and berries. He pretended to reach out and touch them but he never dared. He had cut himself on the leaves once and now won't ever lay finger on the thing. It has become very overgrown. He walks down the slight slope straight ahead and begins humming and whistling 'Le Festin,' but he is unaware the tune even has a name.

A few yards along the way, great patches of light gray asphalt begin to become visible under all the grass and weeds. The patches get big and bigger until they connect together and make a ragged ribbon shape, dotted with faded yellow lines. Simon follows the yellow dots. He always does when he comes this way. Helps keep from getting lost. Along the side of the ribbon of concrete appear little plots of short, dark, greener grass--different grass, not 'wild everywhere' kind of grass. Some patches are little and square, some are long and skinny, some are L-shaped and still others have great deep pits in the middle of them, lined with concrete and stone with flat jagged bits sticking up. They were all different. Simon had been here before. There were pictures here and books and broken bits of glass but Simon had seen all of that before. Made careful mental note of everything interesting.

Simon walked deliberately on, never giving anything more than a passing, disinterested glance. Simon shook his arms as he walked, grimaced a little, but kept his eyes in front of him. It was getting very hot and even more uncomfortable.

The asphalt stopped. Just like that. Dead stop. The plot of grass stopped. Everything stopped. Simon stopped and looked ahead, up the hill. Gravel and muddly bits of large rocks at his feet, Simon began to climb and walk up the side of the hill until he could see the huge red building, sitting like the Pantheon in Rome. Perfect lines of hard red brick, big open wooden doors, huge gasping windows down each side, all lined and trimmed with silver cement and black wrought iron. Massive fat soot-stained smoke stacks, tall streaked chimneys crumbling in on themselves, giant robotic lungs that now roost birds and cover drenched rats' mealy heads. Bits of busted, rusted up machinery, clogged up plumbing and neglected masonry and depilated engineering, bare bones, all putrid, all ghostly, all husk, no kernel. All dead now.

Simon walked through the doors and looked at all the glass smashed on the dirty, hard rock floor, bird poop and dust and loose papers. His little feet made loud slaps on the ground as he walked, eyes up and spinning around, watching and wondering.

His heart was pounding out of his chest.

He could hardly breathe. It was hard to find the air. He picked up a handful of the red dirt. The air inside smelled like bugs to Simon.

He went all the way to the back of the decaying factory and right up to an enormous steel fan. It looked like an extremely powerful exhaust fan and was covered in rust and little drops of condensating liquid. Simon ran his finger along the edge of one of the mean looking blades, examined the liquid and grabbed the lowest blade of the fan and pushed down hard. Whirl. The fan went around, then slowly sputtered and stopped again without much more than a weak gust. Simon grabbed again and pushed doubly hard. And the fan went whirl and sputter sputter, but it took twice the time and a full-on breeze was achieved.

Simon noticed behind the fan was a long chain and series of gears. He noticed the chain touched the black round teeth of each of the gears, all but one. He pulled on the chain to rejoin the two and after much effort it slipped on with a loud thud, but it caught his index finger and pinched it hard, pulled a small bloody chunk out. Simon quickly put the finger in his mouth to soothe it. The blood tasted metallic. Why would it taste metallic? How strange, Simon thought, and then his mind began to drift and he remembered seeing brightly colored pictures in books of creatures called 'Boreas.' Again he was unaware the beings even had a name, but he could tell they had a purpose and that they had a history and that made him want to remember them, and he did. And he imagined other creatures and beings like that and fabulous creations and wondrous far off places. He took his finger out of his mouth and sighed.

   Simon ran around and grabbed the top edge of the fan blade and turned. Whirl. Chunk. Chunk. Chunk. Chug. Air began to surge out. Simon's hair soon went flying every direction and his feet started to slide on the floor without him even picking them up. He put his hand over his eyes as dust and papers began to fly violently everywhere. He had to walk backwards to get out the front of the building that was now being torn apart from the wind. The two big wooden doors had become detached early and went surfing down the hillside. Whole bricks were beginning to come loose from their masonry and shoot like cannons down toward the patches and plots of grass. Simon ran as fast as he could down the strip of yellow lines and dodged behind the hedgerow of his yard, caught his breath, made for the old screen door and shuttered himself in, to wait for the air to even back out, as he was sure it would have to do…

And that is how Simon recalled the wind.

Chapter Four:
Simon Split the Seams

It was hot. The sun felt like it was too close. The ground was baked hard beneath Simon's feet. Dust was everywhere, all over the grass, all over the surface of things, caked on thick. Simon was covered in it. It was in his hair and all down his arms, stuck under his nails. He was sweating. The edges of his hair were wet and clinging to his head. His shirt, damp, also clung to him in uncomfortable patches on his chest and back. The underside of his forearm was marked by little dark brown spots were the sweat and dust had met and commingled. They looked like kingdoms on some old fashioned map.

A skinny half-grown dog walked up, a Boxer mix, mostly red with white spots. It stopped by Simon's feet. Simon looked down at it. He had seen the dog before. The two of them looked out far in front of themselves.

Simon's eyes rested high up on top of a huge mound climbing steadily up from the low grass where they stood. It was one of the highest spots around. You could see almost everywhere from directly on top of it. It was one of the highest spots around. In fact, at the very top it was flat, very flat and long. Very long. A field. Simon hummed. Partly Mozart's Piano Sonata in C major and partly Canon in D by Pachelbel. He was unaware that they were different pieces of music. The dog simply sat down on its bony haunches and panted.

It was so hot.

He strained his eyes. He could see the metal glint. Up on top of the raised field was a series of tall, sturdy metal poles with thin, barely perceptible metal wires strung between them, and caught in the midst of all the metal, being supported, were vast stretches of off white canvas. The canvas sagged in the middle, weighed down by enormous amounts of sloshing, undulating liquid.

Simon walked slowly up the gentle slope, the dog trailing after. He got to the top and arms akimbo, he examined the whole area, tried to reach up and touch the bottom of the sapping cloth, couldn't quite make it. He looked to his left and right, and after a great deal of searching he found a dangerous-looking long piece of half-rusted metal laying errantly on the ground. It appeared to be nearly twice his height when he held it, wobbling, on its end. He brought it back down to Earth with a crackling sound sent the dog running behind a bush, where it looked out timidly. Simon shot it a disapproving look and it inched back out. The top of the piece of metal was sharp. It nicked the tip of Simon's left ring finger. He shook the blood off, watching it fall in sprinkles onto the ground and the lime green shafts of wild grass. It was perfect.

On the bottom of each of the high canvas bags was a dark, thick seam with lots of little white threads poking in and out, some frayed edges that left the very weakest spots exposed. It looked strong but old. Simon picked up the piece of metal underhanded so that the point faced straight up, squinted his eye and yanked up in one sudden movement and…slosh…the whole bag shuddered and waved. He pulled a short spot and out it came, a drop first, then a trickle, as it made its way down the steel stick and hit Simon on the face. He reached out and touched a drop with his two fingers. Water. Perfect. And with an abrupt smile on his face, Simon began to run, slicing down the seams, watching all the little white threads pop and go flying out and the edges of the canvas bag go mad and fluttering like a massive movement of birds' wings.

And every time he finished one section and ran past the metal poles that connected the whole thing with the metal wires, and his pipe hit those pipes, it would make a flash or a spark, and an awful resounding thunder.

And the water poured out, first in torrents and sheets and then in drops and finally a little trickle. It washed the dust off everything.

It was clean.

And finally Simon, screaming and smiling to the end, had opened every bit of cloth on the hill. He was drenched. The air was cool. Simon walked back down the slope with his metal shard in hand, grinning. The dog followed.

And that is how Simon opened the seams of the sky.

Chapter Five:
Ophiuchus and Serpens and Hercules

Not far from Simon's house sat two rather squat but big and proud brick buildings. They were, despite their stocky and utilitarian architecture, very tall, and they were identical in every way from the outside. They both had the same number of floors, the same dimensions--they were perfect shadows of each other. There was a brief space between the two of them but hardly anything could make its way through the narrow path provided. That space was more intended for a variety of odd, esoteric vents and fins and pipes and rusted, charred off, broken shards of metal and glass and wire that seemed to connect the buildings and their environs neatly together. The buildings were crumbling down, the ceilings given way in the middle of both, with a kind of oculus effect when inside. Grasses and bushes sprang up and thrived at the concrete bases and also inside. In fact, inside both buildings was a kind of jungle, even more grown up and untamed than the woods behind Simon's house. There were a series of large open rooms inside, some totally empty, some with piles of waterlogged papers and pots and pans, some with still-shiny but buckled long, hardwood floors.

The room that contained Simon at the time was a very large room on the bottom floor of the building on the left. This room had a number of large maps all along the walls and rows of symbols and drawings and stacks and stacks of books that all contained the same maps and rows and rows of symbols.

Simon sat cross-legged on the dusty floor, a book, open wide, laid across his thighs, his young eyes watching the corner of the room where the thick body of a snake slipped from a hole in the floor, up through a curve and into another room. Simon couldn't see the head or the tail, just the syrupy coils and the tight muscles propelling it. It looked nearly black and with every move it seemed to 'pop'. Simon could figure out the maps well enough. He could divine out his location adequately and he knew that there were few snakes in the area that were known to be dangerous. But Simon had come face to face with a monkey not more than two days ago, and he thought he had known for sure that monkeys were not common…it seemed everything was different than what most of the maps and books suggested. Simon found this puzzling.

The real problem was that in the not-too-distant past, all the zoo and circuses had stopped being…but the animals had not. Simon had no way of knowing any of this.

Simon did, however, understand the animal troubles to be born of his ignorance and not of his stupidity or of some inclement supernatural atmosphere. He was very lucky this way.

Simon's eyes went back to the chart on his lap, a graph of converging lines on a dark blue background with a profuse sprinkling of gleaming white dots and big fiery red orbs, careening comets, collapses and collisions. Little lines drawn between the stars: a scoop, a hunter, a bull. It was starting to get dark outside. Simon turned his eyes to the window and watched for a minute as the orange-red light began to fade.

He slid the book off his lap, walked carefully to the windowpane and touched it. It was cold. He watched the sky for a while and even as the darkness, the deep blues and purple, began to set in, it looked depressingly empty. Vacant. Simon had no place to put his eyes.

He walked half-stomping--the loud noises frightened the animals away before he even got to them. He also hummed and whistled loudly for the same reason. Some animals didn't hear, they only felt. Some animals didn't feel, so much as they heard, so Simon found a wide array for scaring off strange creatures. Flapping one's arms wildly worked well, but sometimes seemed to provoke interest and attention.

He walked to a tall metal cabinet and turned the rusty, downward L-shaped handle and pulled the flimsy door open, slowly. He looked around the door and then quickly flung it open. He pulled out a long sheet of metallic paper, steel gray, and another blood red, sparkling silver and gleaming white and picked up a pair of ancient shears laying on the floor. He began cutting and tearing wildly, making shapes, letting the cast off bits just fall. He made millions of circles, triangles, little dots, things with spines, bits that looked like long teeth, fuzzy globs. He shuffled them all together and tried to pick them up, but there were too many and every time he could get more, more fell out of his clutching arms. He looked around and saw a large glass jar. He grabbed it and the lid laying next to it. He jammed it full of his paper cut-outs, twisted on the lid and began to run outside, thought better of it and slowed down, watching his feet and stomping the whole way out of the room, down the long sinewy hallway. His echoing, stamping feet thundered. He also slapped the cold concrete walls as he went and not until he warily made it out of doors did he begin to run again. But run he did, fast, out of breath and stumbling.

He made it to the top of the stony ridge in front of the longest stretch of unbroken sky he could find. He ran to the very end of it and when he got scared, he laid down on his stomach and inched forward until his head hung over the side. His jar was laying on its side next to him. He reached back and looked out in front of his eyes for a moment, shook the jar and took his arm out from underneath his belly, shifted his weight around, unscrewed the lid and tossed out the cut-outs. A few stuck around the rim and at the very bottom, so he shook the jar hard and flung it outward like trying to fling the last bits of water out of a cup, flinging it dry. The cut-outs bloomed in the air, swirling and spiraling, and finally they slowed and stayed put where they were as if glued. And Simon looked out at them and began connecting them with little white lines in his mind. No scoops or cups or Nimrod-like hunters, no crabs or twins (Simon didn't even know such a thing as twins could happen), but there was a dog and a sunflower and a monkey (Simon was very taken with the monkey) and it was beautiful.

And it was beautiful.

And that is how Simon put stars back in the sky.

And it was never vacant again.

Chapter Six:
Music

Simon sat cross-legged on the slide of a slope, playing with a blade of grass in his hand. Clouds floating in the air above his head, they seemed to bounce.   A clump of trees grew just behind him, the trunks going straight up toward the sun, coming out at weird angles as the earth they grew in graded downward and slanted.   The field in front of his eyes was bright and golden, tall grasses swaying, thick heads of grassy grains bursting, birds landing gracefully and eating and popping back up into the unflappable air.   Closest to him on the weeds were two birds, one blue and brown and the other vivid red.   They had odd skin on their legs, leathery, and it looked like scales.   There was no sound.

A few honeybees flew down and surrounded intensely a large purple bunch of clover.   Simon called bees 'embers' because bees made him seem to want to remember something, and Simon believed the word 'ember' to be the word for remember, because as embers were faintly glowing bits of a once-roaring fire (they can still very much burn you, Simon was aware), so are memories little hot crumbs of ash that refer to another thing or thought. He called 'birds' birds.   The bees hurried away.

Simon watched the way the birds clutched the tops of the tall strands of grass, their little bony toes wrapped around so carefully, hanging their heads down so their sharp little beaks could pluck off the plumpest grains, the way the rigid, thin stem would bend but not break under the little birds' weight.   Everything would spring right back to normal as the birds exploded back into the sky. Simon felt a faint wind blow across his face.   His hair shifted.   He looked up into the breeze. Soft mellifluous air.   But nothing made a sound.   It was silent.

There was a broken clay jar sticking out of the ground not far from his feet, to the left.   The bottom was completely gone, but the dirt and mud clogged up the hole and the handle was cracked off. The wind blew across the top of the jar and made a low resonating sound, and as the breeze shifted around slightly the tone from the jar began to oscillate.   Tiny little vibrations.   Simon got up and walked over to the jar and picked it up.   Muddy dirt and spider webs went everywhere and the noise stopped.   He grabbed a handful of the soft, murky, musical dirt and put it in his pocket, then walked down the slope through the tall grasses, bending them back and leaving a V-shaped path through.   Still holding the broken jar in one hand, arm outstretched, holding the thing far away from his body, he never took his eyes off the chunk of pottery.

On the other side of the field was a tall pile of bright blue plastic pipes,   the symbols 'PVC' stamped at the bottom of each one.   Most of the ones at the top were dry-rotted and sun-bleached and cracking, worthless things that only stained the landscape.   Simon had passed by them almost daily without a thought, except occasionally he wondered how he could get rid of them.   Today was different.

Simon cleared off the top of the pile and collected up the intact pipes--long ones, thick ones, some wide, some narrow.   He put the pot down and dug some (but not all) of the mud out of his pocket, patched up the bottom and pushed a long pipe down into the opening.   He moved the pipe and pot out into the open field and waited for the wind.   Sure enough, the wind came and blew through the pipe and clay jug and made a melodious breathing sound.   Simon rushed back to the other pipes, loaded them into his arms and ran back.   He began jamming pipes together and lashing them into groups with vines or willow branches or whatever he could find.   Noticing that different-sized pipes made different sounds, he would pause at times to let the wind play through one pipe or another, carefully listening to the particular tone before attaching it in its rightful spot on the ever-growing, slightly-leaning, sculpture of sound.   In the middle, facing the wind directly, he had a long pipe with a very wide opening that made a low bellow, and lashed around it were three small pipes that made a lively short sound, like chirp.   He had, going off to the sides, four long, curved pipes that never faced wind directly, and they made a droning, almost incidental, forgetful sound.

And at the very bottom were two very short, very wide pipes that made big barking thuds. There were all kinds of different thuds and crashes and reverberations, and if Simon moved the whole piece carefully around, rotating it slightly in the wind, it would swoosh and jingle and sometimes very nearly breathe. The clay jar beneath buzzed constantly and Simon could feel all the sound and movement in his feet. It all moved through the ground, vibrations, and back up at him like sorcery, like he was some kind of wizard. It made him happy. Simon smiled. He looked at his wind organ and pulled on his ears. The birds flew up and down. The bees buzzed. The air whooshed back and forth and Simon heard it all and everything made a sound and everything was loud.

And this is how Simon discovered music.

And nothing was ever quiet again.

Chapter Seven:
Makers Montagne

Simon pulled the two-wheeled cart with both arms, grunting, sometimes walking backwards, sweat drenching his brow.   The thing was ancient, nothing but two high wheels, one on each side, a flat sheet of wood between them and short planks of wood on three of the four sides to hold things in--in this case dirt--and a long handle with a broken, splintered limb for a grip.   It was a heavy load this time.   He usually liked to move the dirt before there got to be this much of it.   The boards, the pieces of wood, all had strange nail holes in them and had at one time been painted green, but by now most of the paint was gone, peeled off down to the raw bone, yellow wood. When Simon found them they were laying in a field with little bits of grass growing up through the cracks and holes.   Now they are parts of Simon's cart. The wheels pop over the stony ground as he inches upward along the broad side of the slope.   He looks down at the individual rocks and picks up anything that looks of any interest, a certain flatness, a different than usual shade, the edges…he looks for variations, he lifts them up and examines and puts them away in his pockets for closer inspection later.   But not too many, only the best, and maybe not any at all, seeing as this is the sort of thing that gets him into this trouble.   All these heavy loads of rock and dirt and other curiosities that accumulate, after he pockets them and examines them and learns what he can from them, he piles them up in piles, piles that he eventually puts into this cart, this cart he eventually drags along the broad side of the slope and dumps…he hasn't the room at his house to retain all this cast-off junk.   He takes it far behind and into the big open field next to where the slope breaks out in pits, sandy places, and the green muddy bog where it never dries and flies gather, and with a mere twist of the wrist pours large amounts of fine dust, pebbles, rocks and dirt clods held together with bright white tender grass roots.

 This is the project for today.   As he stops to rest and breathe, his ribcage aches from the big breaths, muscles down his sides knotted up and sore.   The skinny dog has returned and follows along at Simon's side, stopping when he does, and tongue draped out of his mouth, begins moving again when Simon does.   Simon doesn't understand why the animal comes so near, nor does he understand what the animal hopes to gain, and he often looks at him suspiciously.   But the truth is, Simon has begun to expect him, a new variation.

They both walk, Simon yanking suddenly on the split wooden handle.   The wheels begin to slowly roll with a groan.   Both dog and boy look straight ahead from under heavy, rumpled foreheads with the occasional look up at a certain ambulating cloud or behind to make such no dirt is lost in the jostle and rustle of the trip.

The dog puts his nose to the ground and gets distracted by diverse and dissimilar scents such as decaying mole, mildewed leaves, animal excrement.   He follows the smells along spiraling paths, excitedly yapping and flapping his tail and, ultimately finding all unreliable, returns quickly to Simon's side.

Simon has been watching the dog's behavior.

When they finally reach a spot from which they can adequately dispose of the dirt, Simon quickly turns the cart on its side and begins shaking the wooden sides to liberate any dust or stones stuck in the thick cracks along the bottom and joints, puts the cart back upright and looks down.   But 'down' isn't very far down anymore and in fact it is 'up', having ceased to be a pit and now more of an allover heap or mount.   Several large peaks are starting to birth themselves, high craggy things in the midst of dropped off dust.   And some of the litter and debris has been washed down by rain and in some thick gelatinous stage dried and formed wide bases around everything, the dog went down there to investigate but Simon just watched, having neither the nerve nor the shoes for the job (barefoot as he is).   And all along the sides of everything are different colors, different shades all dependant upon what new and exciting color or texture had particularly excited Simon that week or month or day.   The different layers of color and form looked like striation.   Simon was making mountains.   Simon and the dog were making mountains.   Simon looked contently at the heaps and piles, arms akimbo.   He grinned at the dog and they both began making their way back to the house to pile on another load.

Chapter Eight:
Aeschylus and the Whole Universe

It had been morning and then without much notice it became afternoon but all of that is gone now and dusk is creeping softly in. The ceruleans and the vermilions that collect along the edges of horizon were already seeping up the sky. The moon was out but it was low. The air was a kind of grey, not much light.

Earlier today, sometime between bright morning and searing afternoon, Simon had made his way back to the two weed-covered buildings. He stood in front, tremors going up and down his whole body. He waited for courage. Courage not coming, he decided speed would have to do. He caught his breath and tried to calm his nerves. Simon was, in fact, scared to go into any structure, but oddly enough not at all frightened once inside. Just the act of entering made him nervous. He seemed such a violent thing. He felt he was invading something or disrespecting some sanctity. He opened his eyes as large as he could and held his breath and rubbed his feet on the ground.

He ran in and grabbed the top half of a tall stack of books he had been eyeing for some time, put them under his arm and quickly ran out again. This was the first time Simon had attempted to take a book away from any of the buildings. He was apprehensive. He wasn't completely sure what had occurred that had left this world the way it was…something had occurred, that much was obvious. Big buildings, small buildings, buildings with doors fluttering in the stiff wind, shiny pieces of metal left scattered about, whole panes of glass shattered, windows open, books laid out, cracks down the spines, loose pages flapping in the breeze. He was anxious about what he touched and what he took with him. Dirt or flowers or rocks were one thing, but the manufacture of this planet frightened him slightly.

Earlier when it was day, Simon made his way hastily home, three thick books in tow. He ran inside his house and slammed the tomes down on a table, staring at them for a while. The first one, pale white and gold, read 'Classical Greek Drama, Aeschylus, Sophocles and Euripides.' The second one, even bigger than the first, was black and brown and read 'Fifty tales of Gods and Goddesses of Classical Mythology' and finally, a thin little volume in silver and white that said simply 'Sappho Lyrics'. Simon couldn't read a word of any of that, however, and he simply put them next to each other and flipped through the pages of all three books simultaneously, absorbing the little fiery symbols flying off the pages and the big painted color plates and illustrations of fairy tales, Greek chorals, urns, flowers, beasts, trees, amphitheatres, shiny marble bits of antiquity. His face shining with joy.

Simon walked over to his big window and touched the thick white drapery, rubbed it between his fingers. Grabbed a big clutch of fabric and pulled and pulled, jumped up and tried to liberate the drapery every way he could, and finally, with a fatalistic rip, it all came tumbling down on him in a big folded pool. Simon stood up in the middle of the curtain, grabbed two equal ends of it and began to wrap himself, tucking corners in, pulling out stray pieces, until he was completely wrapped in the thing. He walked to the last room of the house and grabbed an ugly, worn out holiday wreath with huge bare gaps in it and placed it squarely on his head.

Simon walked outside. He had discovered imagination.

Simon began to give speeches, monologues…to everything. He spoke to the trees. He spoke to the little red dog. He taught the birds in the trees. He expanded on difficult measures of morality with the crayfish…or attempted to as they scurried backwards down their adobe chimneys. He preached on indispensable kinds of dignity to the herd of feral cattle that passed through weekly in the low field behind the house. He instructed a line of ants carrying crumbs as he sat on the sandy edge of the creek on the importance of leisure and charity. The trees he taught to be more gentle, more visionary, more expressive.

They fluttered their leaves knowingly.

But now that it was getting late, the ants were gone. Lightning bugs flew around his head, showering everything with blinking yellow. The sky was pale purple. He was tracing the ant line now with a stick, casually. The dog yipped and vainly jumped around trying to catch the glowing bugs. When he finally succeeded he coughed madly and spit and spit until he spit it out and then pawed at the crushed body with a confused paw. The dog stopped chasing the lightning bugs.

The trees shook with the evening breeze. Big feathery leaves and petals everywhere and soft tender grass creeping up to the border of sand. Simon twisted his fingers around a loose weed and tapped his stick against a huge fallen hollow tree, whole segments of dead wood cascading off the thing each time Simon absentmindedly drummed at it.

He looked up to the sky and looked at the moon. It was a half moon. Simon drew in the sand a half moon shape. It surprised him. He had no idea he could recreate actual shapes. The half-moon shape was like night, the drawing he made could mean night. It meant night to him…but night is only half the time. The other half is bright. Simon made another drawing. This time he drew two half moons, but they didn't look good so he turned a bit and drew the two half moons together, two halves to make a whole. It looked like a sun. He had surprised himself again. The sun symbol could mean day or sun or everything, but it meant 'day' to Simon, whole day and sunny time of day instead of moon time of day…which was half of the symbol. Simon was amazed and very pleased. He grinned and stood up off the sandy bank and walked back to his house, robe and wreath still hanging heroically off his shoulders and head.

Because he had just discovered writing.

And this is how Simon restarted imagination.

Chapter Nine:
Il Cimitero

Sometimes it was all Simon could do to just hold his breath in this wondrous world. Breeze blowing over him, lifting his hair, late summer evening breeze, kind of warm, kind of orange and red like the stripes and bulges along the horizon. Sometimes he could hardly breathe. He worried he would breathe it in, even a little bit, and he was no worthy receptacle for all the beauty he saw. Even the smallest bit would probably explode him. It pressed down on him from outside, the joy, the splendor. His skinny legs shook. There was a lot to see, you just have to be alive enough to see it.

Beyond a long low golden-yellow field was the tall steep hill, dark green in contrast. The sides of the hill were so steep, in fact, they appeared to slightly bow, so that it seemed that the very top was wider and more bulbous than the approaches. It looked like a big pinch had been grabbed and yanked upward by some bored or malicious giant.

Simon had walked for most of the afternoon through the long empty field, little sharp sticks poking his feet, tough brush getting crushed and bent as he walked scrambling over it. He made wide strides and jumped over whole sections too muddy or brambly to easily transverse. Simon grabbed at the tops of bushy grasses, seed pots hanging loosely down the sides of thorny twigs. He paused to look over interesting variations in the shade or the placement of mud or a grouping of particular plants, the way the sun shone through different old rotten leaves. He found an old, half-decayed clump of waterlogged magazine sticking up out of the ground, picked it up and knocked mud off. He held it out under the sun and looked at the pictures: people sitting around tables sipping drinks from low cups, light tan buildings in the background collecting heat and sunshine, shiny metal glinting in the light. The letters above read, 'Tangiers'. Simon couldn't read it. Simon didn't know what Tangiers was, so it didn't matter. He put the magazine under his arm and kept walking.

As he made his way up the hill, one thing that became noticeable was that the ground was softer and covered more evenly with shorter grasses…and vines. There were a lot of vines growing this way and that and back on themselves, snaking and spiraling everywhere, dark rich dirt spilling out underneath with moss-covering trailing behind. Little powder blue flowers started to make sporadic appearances.

Simon came upon a semi-circle of rusted red spikes punching through the ground and forming a sort of fence. They looked like teeth. He walked up and touched the fence; it was cold. He found it confusing. He walked on and just over the horizon he saw a tree, a big tree, the only tree on the hill. It was, more or less, growing completely out of the very center and its big branches and leaves shaded everything.

After the fence, Simon noticed a flat series of grey rocks traveling in a straight line towards the tree. He walked on them, and soon he noticed another series going the other direction, and then another and another. These pathways were going everywhere.

He saw birds in the sky. He saw bugs on the ground: ants, beetles, butterflies…whole clouds of them, bright blue and yellow in front of him. The clouds above were thin stripes of white wisps, mist in the dark blue atmosphere, dark indigo blue and getting darker as the breeze began to blow cooler and cooler.

Simon rubbed his arm with his hand, friction, to warm himself a bit. He breathed a huge gust of air out to see if he could see it. He couldn't…it wasn't quite that cool. He walked on a while.

It wasn't long before he came to the big slabs of cold rock. Soon, he found himself surrounded by huge monolithic slabs, granite, marble, shorter thinner ones, broken ones, busted up concrete ones, some tiny…just little piles of rocks. Simon's eyes bugged out of his head. His mouth dropped open. He ran around touching them. They were all cold. They entwined with the little stone paths and everything sat neatly under the cover of the gigantic tree in the center. Some of the slabs weren't slabs at all, but were long rectangular boxes, but these were still cold but smooth. Simon ran his fingertips over the tops and finally laid his hands palms down on the surface, and that is when he noticed something, two things really…one, that he could slightly see himself reflected in the surface (but that was little astonishment, lots of things cast reflections back) but the second thing, the second thing gave him quite the turn. He saw symbols etched deeply into the tops of the boxes and on the fronts of the slabs.   All kinds of symbols, numbers (but he didn't know they were called numbers) and letters (but again, he didn't know they were called letters).   Simon jumped back in a start. He put his hand up over his mouth, instinctively. He had to remember to breathe, he **had** to **make himself** remember to breathe. He walked backwards over an ancient rosebush, its brambly strands latching onto his clothes and skin and pulling and ripping.   Simon didn't notice, not even when little dots of dark crimson blood started to pop up in neat little lines up and down his arms and legs. He nearly fell backwards and would have slid down the hillside but he stopped himself, steadying himself by grabbing a long, jutting tree branch. He dropped the magazine. The dark grey bark was rough and under every snag and shabby piece was a thick white tangle of spider webs and dust.

He sat down on the ground and looked at the vines climbing up the tree and up the stones and slabs, his hand still on his mouth.

He closed his eyes.

He opened his eyes and looked out over the field and avoided everything else. He stared and stared out toward the horizon. He didn't make a sound. He sat perfectly still and didn't make a sound and waited. He watched the sun fall further below the sky. He looked at the colors, identified each shade and where he had seen it before. He sat perfectly still and didn't make a sound and he watched the sun go down and he lowered his hand from his mouth and he waited.

Chapter Ten:
Simon and the Standing Stones

He studied the sky talmudically . Every wisp of cloud he observed and every large patch of brilliant blue he measured. He watched the sunlight stream down in big wide swathes and hit the top of the tree leaves and filter through, broken into little reflective shards of almost glass, raining between the foliage like water or mist. A small flying bug not far beyond his face caught his attention, a dragon fly or damsel fly, lace-icicle wings sparkling in the daylight. He held his hand under it and let it cast blurry stained glass-colored shadows on his palm and face. He looked down at his feet and noticed his shadow in the dirt and how it leaked and lurched slightly past the tree line where he stood and out into the high flat field that lay directly past the tree-crowned hill. He kicked the dust at his feet but the black shade remained, so it was not a stain or discoloration. He bent down to look at it closer. It moved. It took his shape again. Him crouching. Around him, he noticed the thick black lines like trunks capped with wide fluffy coronets extending out past the trees. He looked back up into the sky and held his hand out in front of his body and watched the inky fingers of the thing move as he moved, a kind of nighttime behind an object held out into the daytime.

He held a tall stick up and looked at the long thin shadow it created and how it moved as he moved the stick around and as he moved around the stick. The field was a stony one with slate and limestone everywhere, large specimens jutting right out of the ground in places. Simon walked out into the field, past the skeletal remains of an old red tractor sitting, sinking derelict into the dirt, rusting away and taking on a monstrous appearance. The grill in front was chipped and broken away and the effect was such that it seemed to have a big gaping maw of evil broken teeth. Simon was slightly afraid of it and passed it as little as possible. Today he went by it without even looking at it. In fact, he turned his face to the side and deliberately looked at a flowering weed or grass off to his left until he was sure it was far behind him. He walked up to the spot where the limestone stood and carefully studied the shadows around it. He touched the stones and pushed one lightly, surprised to find that it moved in a chunky, gritty kind of way. Intrigued, he pushed harder until it stood completely straight and high. It cast a most magnificent kind of shadow to Simon's eyes. Long and thick and regal. He was quite taken with the effect and soon began to endeavor to raise up all the stones and, when he had finished the task, decided that they should be arranged, haphazard as they were, they cast contrary shades and canceled the other and with a little bit of art the image could be magnified. Simon pushed and tugged at the rough, unhewn, tall bits of native limestone and slate until he had a large ring of eleven big obelisks, all casting deep dark hints across the length of the meadow. He went to the middle and stacked up, in a careful pile, some of the smaller and fat rocks. He walked back and looked it all over but he was not pleased. It did not look right. It looked off balance. Oblong. He scanned around his feet and over his shoulders and finally, far back towards where he had come from, he saw a towering tooth of limestone sticking out of the dusty ground. He walked to it. Pushed on it. Pulled on it. Sweat dripping into his eyes. And he eventually freed it. He moved it slowly, it was heavy. He made his way to his circle and, with much effort, succeeded in finding a place for it and setting it in and upright, stood back quickly to observe it.

As soon as he stood back an odd feeling came over him. The air felt strange and the shadows cast around the bottom of the stones began to behave in an odd way, they began to grow and grow quickly and they branched out in every direction, not just the one as before. Simon looked up towards the sky and the clouds began to race across the blue expanse and before long the very sky itself appeared to move. The wind picked up and was blowing hard and all around in every direction, Simon struggled to stand up, his clothes and hair flying and flinging all around him. The night sky came up and the daytime vanished. The stars came out and rushed about the sky madly, never settling into their natural places. The moon came up in an instant and as quickly fell away again, followed by another blue sunny sky followed by more starry night. Simon watched with wonder. The whole time music played in his head, Ein Kleine Nachtmusik, Mozart. He knew the music because he had found an old cheap music box that played it and he had brought it home with him. He kept it near where he slept at night, next to a fake plastic Tiki lantern with a broken top he used to hold the interesting bird feathers he found daily.   There were no interesting bird feathers out here.   He had looked.   Only interesting happenings now.   He stood as tall and straight as the stones he had set and watched the skies scramble and shimmy, his mouth agape.   At last it began to slow and the last night sky dripped and drifted away back behind the horizon and the sun slowed in relation, but still rather quickly went sailing along the heaven's edge before halting in place.   Late afternoon.

There was a rustling all around him, a big rustle and before long he saw the weeds and grass start to bow down and sway as a blast of breeze rushed upon him.   A cool, almost cold breeze instead of the hot air he was used to, it flung itself around him and left his skin all goosebumped and tight and he turned to watch it run up the tree trunks and fly fluttering through their canopies.   It made the loudest noise and as it rustled the trees, each green leaf it touched and tousled turned a dark gold or yellow or a bright scarlet red.   And all that was an hour before a yawning green or burnt brown or a lifeless grey, was now the color of fire or bright sunlight.   And everything that was sweaty before was now chilly and felt very much like evening.   Simon ran his fingers along the cold stone of the obelisks he had set up and walked back to the house without even noticing the old tractor on his way.

And this is how Simon restarted the passage of time.

Chapter Eleven:
Simon al Vacio

It was barely morning and the sky was still very dark. Simon sat on a thick wooden windowsill, looking out, waiting for the sunrise. He drew in the condensation on the pane: the dog, a sun, some symbols he saw under a picture of a baby in the other room of the house, symbols he had rightly divined spelled out his name as he had also deduced the picture was of him. A person always seems to recognize themselves. The sky was misty but he knew the sun would soon burn that away. He had barely slept the night before and when he did, he had vivid dreams, disturbingly vivid. Long glass windows and long busy streets, light grey concrete and tangles of people, people he had never seen. Mountains, volcanoes, pretty women smiling, automobiles. And when he didn't sleep and dream, he was awake thinking thoughts.

He knew he was going to leave the house today and not come back for a long time, possibly forever. He continued to traces S's in the dew-covered window, big S's, little S's. He quickly and lightly dotted his row of I's, climbed down out of the window seat and walked through all the rooms of his house. He grabbed his thick black glasses that he tried never to wear, but he knew he would need them, pocketed clumps of little plastic sandwich bags, never know when you might need those, some bread ties, a roll of tape, three pens and a notebook, and a small knife.

He stepped out his door and let it slam heavily behind him. He didn't even look back at the noise. His face was grim but resolute.   The air had a definite chill to it.   It was early in the day but late in the season.   He buttoned up his long-sleeved blue shirt and walked.   He walked over all the common hills and slopes.   He went down into the little gullies and valleys between the rises, where all the rain collected into mossy water and all the frogs lived.   He went straight across the long plains and flat places.   Somewhere along the way he acquired the attention of the dog and now it followed along with him.   He passed the big open pits and the library and the wind barn and he scrambled and trekked down the cracked, chunked up bits of grey and yellow concrete, around big broken spires of glass and steel hanging helplessly out of the surrounding, suffocating earth.   He stepped over huge gouges and deep holes, swam across a few stretches of water and waded a few others.   He let the grass tickle his bare feet and he never thought too hard and he didn't make much sound.   And eventually he reached the end of anything familiar.   There wasn't much grass or other greenery left as he walked on, just a lot of dust, and it soon got thicker and thicker and piled up into hills.   Soon there were more and more hills and the hills got higher and higher.   Simon saw a piece of paper flapping in the distance, trapped under a relatively short pile of dust and sand.   He walked towards it and noticed how it fluttered and flailed like some bird or something wounded, but it wasn't an animal, just another loose scrap of paper, a magazine photo.   It was of 'La Primavera' by Botticelli, but Simon didn't know that.   In fact, it didn't even say that on this particular bit of waxy paper, but instead above it said "Our Great Awakening".   It was from a story not about Botticelli or the work itself, but about the Renaissance and the Uffizi.   Simon thought the picture was wonderful.   He folded it up and stuffed it into the already crammed-full pockets of his shorts.

As Simon passed through this increasingly dirty and dusty land, he noticed the heat, it was overwhelming.   He also noticed the Sun.   It had become unrelenting.   There were posts and poles sticking lifelessly out of the ground everywhere.   They were weathered and petrified.   Some were huge and tall and some broken and thin and short.   Some had wide tops that held signs but most all of it was faded and chipped and unreadable.   Soon, most of the land leveled out except for a series of very tall, dune-like hills, two long lines almost equal on both sides of Simon.   He began to walk down through the middle of them.   He found it to be thick and quiet and uncomfortable in the valley.   He noticed, along the high sides of the dunes next to him, pieces of glass and steel sticking through, curved, frosted hunks of glass and polished, chromed metal.   The glint hurt his eyes.   But on top of each dune was a sign, a single sign that looked much newer than the others and much less haphazard.   Each hill had a sign on it that had been placed specially…he began to read them and pay attention to the series. He didn't understand the symbols or the words but the first one read:

In The

And the others continued:

Beginning

All Was

Unformed

And

Was Void.

And past the last hill with the last sign with the last word was nothing but flat open land, burnt to a crisp, cracked and broken in the evil radiating sun.   Simon looked out and, shading his eyes with his hand, walked down the loose slope of the last hill into the void.

www.ingramcontent.com/pod-product-compliance
Lightning Source LLC
Chambersburg PA
CBHW041031170626
46815CB00001B/53